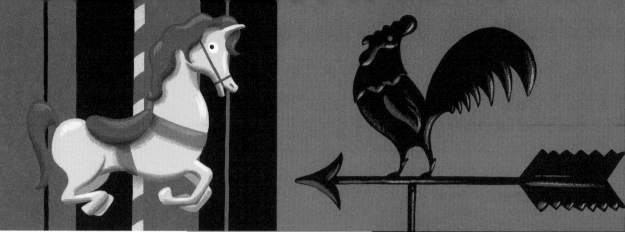

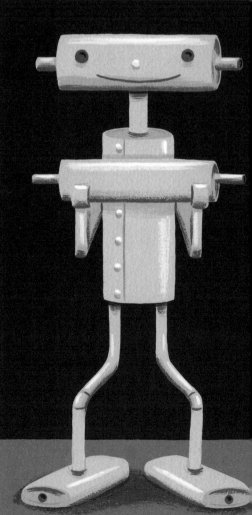

Lawn to Lawn

DAN YACCARINO

Dragonfly Books ——🪰 New York

"I can't wait to move to our new home!" said Pearl.
Betty, Flo, Norm, and Jack weren't so sure. They'd
never even left the lawn before. But they all loved
Pearl, and where she went, they wanted to go too.

Moving day came. Pearl's parents had packed up everything
in the house, but in the confusion, they left a few things behind.
"I may be wrong," said Norm. "But I think they forgot us."
"What'll we *do*?" squawked Flo.

"If we stay here," said Betty, "the new owners may store us in the garage—or, worse . . ."

"THE CURB!" they all said.

"And once the trash truck takes a lawn ornament," declared Jack, "it *never* comes back."

"We have to find Pearl," said Jack. "Let's *go*!"

"Hey—a map," said Betty. "It looks like Pearl's moving to a place called Ritzy Estates. It looks far."

Flo didn't know what she was more afraid of—leaving the lawn or being left behind.

"Well," said Norm, "have a good trip. See you when you get back."

They had to remind him that he was coming with them.

The ornaments set off, following the map, but they hadn't gotten very far when they heard a familiar rumble and wheeze. "Trash truck!" honked Flo.

They all froze. Only Pearl knew that they were real. They'd have to be careful. Some people didn't love lawn ornaments the way Pearl did.

One dark day, they found themselves lost.

"Do you need directions?" asked a garden gnome.

"Why, yes we do!" said Norm.

"What a coincidence!" replied the gnome. "So do we!"

Gnomes weren't great with maps.

So Betty and Jack told the gnomes where to go and plotted a new route for themselves.

The road was rough, but the ornaments were careful and always kept a lookout for the dreaded trash truck.

They had just climbed a tall building to figure out where they were when a gang of creepy gargoyles started following them. Luckily, a brave moose statue chased them away.

"How can I ever thank you?" asked Betty, her heart all aflutter.

"Think nothing of it, ma'am!" said the moose.

The ornaments traveled through swamps and fields.
They climbed buildings and mountains. But they still
had a long way to go.

"Why don't y'all stay here with us, honey?" asked a friendly pink flamingo. "Thanks, doll," said Flo. "But we have a little girl who's expecting us."

The ornaments missed Pearl something awful.
"Watch out for the trash truck!" said the flamingo as the
ornaments hit the road once more.

They were nearing their destination when they heard the roar of a crowd. "A racetrack!" shouted Jack. "Look at those jockeys ride!"

Jack felt a powerful urge to stay, but Betty just looked at him and said, "Remember Pearl." And they were on their way.

After miles and trials, they finally made it to Ritzy Estates. But —

"Where do you think *you're* going?" snarled a snooty lion.
"Yeah! No one gets past *us*," growled another. "Beat it!"

The ornaments slumped to the curb in despair.

"We came so far only to be turned away," sighed Betty.

"Pearl's probably forgotten all about us by now, anyway," said Flo.
They were so sad that they didn't hear the familiar rumble and wheeze.

And before they knew it, they were tossed into the back of a trash truck!

"We're going to the junkyard!" cried Flo.
"I guess this is it," said Betty.

Then Norm giggled.

"What are *you* so happy about?" asked Jack.

Norm smiled and pointed. "Look!"

They were driving right through the gates of Ritzy Estates,
and there was nothing those lions could do about it!

"Pearl, here we come!" shouted Jack.

And then—there she was! The ornaments hopped down and ran to her.

"I *knew* you'd come!" Pearl cried. "I missed you so much. Thank goodness you're home."

And Jack, Betty, Flo, and even Norm knew the journey had been worth it. They were where they belonged, with their Pearl, once more.

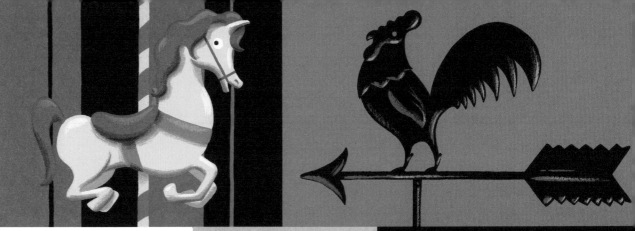

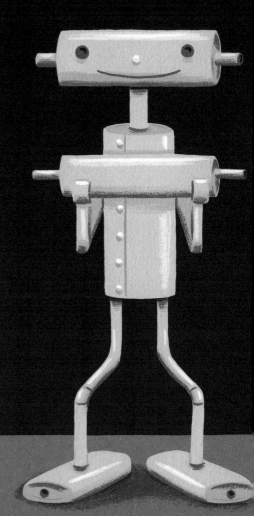